I Have It!

by Mickey Daronco

I have a tan cat.
My tan cat is fat.
My cat is on the mat.

I have a can.
I put my can in a pan.
The pan is not hot yet.

I have a big bag.
My bag is red.
My red bag has a tag.

I have a fan.
I put my fan in a van.
I will go home with it.

I have a map.
I set my map on my lap.
I look at the map.

I have a bat.
I put my cap on my bat.

I put my cap on me!